FEB 1 2 2019

P9-CLI-162

MICHAEL DAHL PRESENTS

SCREAMS IN SPACE 4D

HAUNTED PLANET

BY AILYNN COLLINS
ILLUSTRATED BY JUAN CALLE

STONE ARCH BOOKS
a capstone imprint

Michael Dahl Presents is published by Stone Arch Books,
A Capstone Imprint
1710 Roe Crest Drive
North Mankato, Minnesota 56003
www.mycapstone.com

Summary: After years of traveling through space, a crew of humans has finally found an empty
world to make their home. But after almost twelve-year-old twins Evie and Emery Linn sneak
down to the surface, Evie starts noticing troubling signs. Plants curl tightly around her finger.
Strange tracks lead into a dark cave. Evie can't help but wonder—are they truly alone on this
planet? Download the Capstone 4D app to access a variety of bonus content.

Library of Congress Cataloging-in-Publication Data is available on the Library of Congress website.

ISBN: 978-1-4965-7904-1 (library hardcover)
ISBN: 978-1-4965-7908-9 (ebook PDF)

Printed and bound in the USA.
PA48

1 Ask an adult to
download the app.

 Capstone 4D
Education

2 Scan any page with the star.

3 Enjoy your cool stuff!

————— OR —————

Use this password at capstone4D.com

planet.79041

MICHAEL
DAHL
PRESENTS

Michael Dahl has written about werewolves, magicians, and superheroes. He loves funny books, scary books, and mysterious books. Every Michael Dahl Presents book is chosen by Michael himself and written by an author he loves. The books are about favorite subjects like monster aliens, haunted houses, farting pigs, or magical powers that go haywire. **Read on!**

INTO THE DARK . . .

When I look at the night sky, I wonder—
does scary stuff happen up there just
as it does here on Earth? Sounds can't
travel through outer space because
there's no air. So if frightened people
were out there, we'd never even hear
their screams. I wonder . . .

In *Haunted Planet*, a crew of humans
is traveling through space, looking for
a new home. And they think the planet
named AX-351 might be it. But when
twins Evie and Emery visit the alien
world, they discover weird, deadly
plants that will do anything to survive.
Anything. And then they see the ghosts.

Michael Dahl

"Emery, there's life down there!" Evie Linn said. She waved her twin brother over to her side. "Tell me these aren't animal tracks."

Evie was squinting at a hologram floating above the computer panel. The 3-D image showed the surface of the new planet below them.

The crew of their ship, the *Wanderer*, had been studying this strange, new world named AX-351. Scientists had been gathering info on it for the last twenty star-days. Now, they were ready to go to the surface in small groups called away teams.

"They're not animal tracks," Emery said robotically. He kept his eyes glued to his computer station.

"You didn't even look," Evie said with a huff.

Emery glanced up long enough to scowl at his sister. "Stop bugging me," he said. "You know I'm preparing to be on that first away team. I need to be the first crew member to catalog ten alien plant species. I have to win the internship."

Evie rolled her eyes. Of course she knew. Winning the year-long internship with the ship's chief botanist had been Emery's dream since he was six.

Evie crossed the small space that was the living room section of their home quarters. She had her TAB portable computer in her hand. She stuck it between her brother's face and his computer station.

"Look!" she demanded. She swished her hand over the image, zooming in. "There! See how those holes in the ground repeat and make a pattern? They have to be animal tracks."

Annoyed, Emery stood up and faced his twin. Even though he was born three minutes before Evie, she was half a head taller. They both had the same black hair and brown eyes, but Emery had specks of green in his eyes, just like their mother's.

"Let it go!" Emery said. "Every scientist on this ship has been studying the planet. They all agree—there's no animal life."

"That's not possible," Evie argued. "If a world has this many plants, something must live on it. It only makes sense."

"And yet our best minds have determined that there is none," Emery replied. "You're just imagining these mystery creatures."

Emery returned to his work. Evie stared at his back for one long minute before returning to her own station. She had sat at this station every day for the last six years, studying and doing assignments. But finally, she was done.

Now that she was about to turn twelve, Evie would join the ship's crew as a full working member. She only had one more step to take. She had to decide which three ship departments she'd like to join. Then she'd take their tests and wait for a job offer from one. She would serve with that department for the rest of her life.

That was how things worked aboard the *Wanderer*, for all three thousand people who lived on the huge ship. Only, Evie couldn't decide which three departments to pick.

For Emery, the choice had been easy. He'd always wanted to join the botany department. He loved plants and had easily aced their test.

Evie, on the other hand, was average at every subject. She loved reading, though, and she loved writing her own stories. But on the *Wanderer*, there was no department that needed stories.

"You know . . . ," she said to Emery. She heard him sigh, but she went on. "Humans have been taking land away from animals and other humans for thousands of years. They destroyed others' homes to build their own. That created tons of problems, like starting wars and spreading disease. Whole plant and animal species have died out. Shouldn't we at least try not to make the same mistake?"

Emery leaned back in his chair and crossed his arms. "Ev, when we were little, I loved the stories you made up. You could imagine the wildest things. It was fun."

He walked over to his sister and looked at the image she was studying. He saw no signs of life.

"But we're not kids anymore," Emery said. "We need to focus on our survival. AX-351 is the first planet we've found that humans might actually be able to live on. It's the best chance we have for a new home. Don't ruin it with your imaginary fears. OK?"

"This isn't one of my stories, Em," Evie said. She hated that he didn't believe her. "If we take over someone else's planet without permission, we're asking for trouble."

Emery patted his twin on her shoulder. "Everything will be all right. You'll see."

2

The alarm beeped for end of study time. Right on schedule, the door to the twins' home quarters slid open. Their parents walked in, looking tired.

In space there was no day and night. So whenever their parents were working, Evie and Emery would study. When their parents returned, they'd have dinner and free time before bed.

It was Emery's turn to prepare their meal. He pulled out four small packets and placed them in an oven-like machine. In just a few minutes, the packets would turn into four servings of spaghetti.

While the meals cooked, Evie started clearing the table. Their parents went into their room to change out of their uniforms.

Their mom was a botanist, and their dad worked on the bridge—the part of the ship that piloted them through space. Like everyone else on the *Wanderer*, they worked ten ship-hours on duty and had fourteen ship-hours off. Dinner was usually a time for the twins to catch up on what was happening on the *Wanderer*. Tonight, their parents were especially excited.

"All our drones have returned to the ship," Dad said as he dug in to his spaghetti. "The information they've collected proves that AX-351 is safe."

"Which means we're finally ready to send teams to the surface!" Mom said. "Some teams will continue to perform studies. Others will start to build temporary shelters."

"Yes! I knew it!" Emery said, pumping his fist. Mom and Dad laughed. Evie chewed on her food in silence.

"We spent our entire shift loading up the cargo barges," Mom continued. "The first team heads down in a few hours. My team leaves tomorrow."

"You mean *our* team, don't you?" Emery said. He beamed. He was so excited, he had barely eaten any of his food. "I'm ready to join the botany department and serve with you, Mom!"

Mom gave Dad an odd look. Evie watched her parents carefully. She knew there was something they weren't saying. Emery was talking too much to notice.

"I'm all caught up on the plant life on this world," Emery went on. "I'm sure I'm going to win that internship." He started to stand to grab his TAB, but then Dad spoke up.

"Crew, you aren't going to like this," he said. Whenever Dad had bad news, he called them *crew* instead of *kids*. "The captain has decided that only adults will be allowed on the planet for now. We're still checking the air quality. Once the temporary shelters are up and sealed from the planet's atmosphere, everyone will be able to come down."

"But we *are* adults," Emery said. "We're twelve."

"Almost twelve," Mom reminded him. "You still have another seven ship-days before you're both fully twelve Earth years old."

"That's nothing," Emery said. "We're twelve because we finished our finals."

"Evie hasn't done her final tests," Dad said, frowning at the twins.

Evie shrunk in her seat.

Emery glared at his sister. "She just doesn't know where she wants to be assigned yet," he replied. "That's all."

"I don't know why we still keep our clocks on Earth time," Evie said, hoping to change the subject. "Nobody on the *Wanderer* has even seen Earth. It seems like an outdated way of keeping time, don't you think?"

Nobody answered Evie. The rest of the family was too busy arguing. Emery insisted on going down to the planet. Their parents said he needed to stay aboard the ship.

Finally, Dad had heard enough. He slapped his hand on the small dining table, making it wobble.

"Captain's orders cannot be disobeyed!" Dad said. "It's for your own safety. There is so much that we still don't know about AX-351. Let those with experience check it out first."

"No one has experience—" Emery started to argue.

But Dad stood up, and that meant no more discussion.

Emery stomped his way back to his bedroom. Evie followed. No one had finished their meal.

"You'll be able to go down in just over a week," their mom called. "And, Em, if you don't win the internship, there's always next year."

In Emery's room, Evie studied her brother's sketches of flowers, seeds, shrubs, and trees that he'd stuck all over the walls. Emery sat on the floor beside his bed, stewing in anger.

"Mom is right, Em," Evie said. "Besides, the teams will probably find something wrong, and we'll move on to another planet. This might just be another dud."

"It's taken three generations to find a planet we can live on," Emery said. "This has to be the one. It has water, gravity, a similar atmosphere to Earth, and even plants! It's just my bad luck. I wanted to be the youngest crew member ever to win the internship with the chief botanist."

Evie joined her twin on the floor. They sat in silence for a long time. Then Emery looked over at his sister with a sparkle in his eye.

"Evie," he said. "How would you like a chance to prove there's life on the planet?"

"What do you mean?" Evie said, frowning. Emery's ideas usually got the twins into trouble.

"Let's sneak out on the first barge tonight," Emery said. "I'll help you look for life, if you help me collect plants. All I need are ten samples. I'll be able to work on them right here." He jumped to his feet. "I'll win the internship for sure!"

Evie stared at her brother as he began gathering his equipment. Sneaking off the ship was a very dangerous thing to do. But if there really was animal life on the planet, the *Wanderer* crew couldn't just move in. Evie thought back to the stories she'd read of ancient humans—how they had taken over others' homes and caused so much death and hurt.

Evie had no choice. She couldn't let the *Wanderer* accidentally destroy innocent creatures. She had to find out the truth about what was on the planet. Even if it meant getting into the worst trouble of her life.

3

Sneaking out of their home quarters was easy. Mom and Dad had already gone to bed and sealed their room. Their parents wouldn't hear a thing.

Getting onto a barge was the hard part. First, Emery and Evie removed their locator badges and left them in their beds. Anyone looking for them would think they were in their rooms. Then they grabbed their life-packs. Inside were Spaceskins, which were suits they needed anytime they went off the ship. The packs also held food and water, research equipment, and basic first-aid supplies.

The twins swung the life-packs onto their backs and headed for the launch bay. It was located at the very back of the *Wanderer*. Walking there on a regular day would've taken fifteen minutes. Sneaking there took almost an hour. The twins had to avoid other crew members by ducking into empty rooms and elevators.

Emery and Evie slipped through a side door and into the launch bay. It was the largest room on the ship and big enough to hold seven huge spacecrafts for carrying cargo, called star-barges. It also stored four smaller ships that carried crew only and a special ship used by the captain.

The twins ducked behind a large crate as on-duty crew walked by. They were busy loading equipment and boxes into the star-barges. Hover technology helped the process go faster. The heavy equipment floated inches above the floor, making it easier for the crew to move them.

"How are we going to get past so many people and onto the star-barge?" Emery whispered.

Evie didn't answer right away. She was looking at the huge crate they were crouched behind. She could just make out an outline of a small rectangle in the crate's smooth surface.

"Em, I think this part of the crate has an opening so the crew can check what's inside," she said. "We might be able to get through it."

With her fingertips, Evie pulled the rectangle open. It was just big enough for her head to fit.

"We'll have to separate our pack into parts to get our stuff through," Evie whispered, opening up her life-pack. She threw her belongings in one at a time and then squeezed herself inside.

"Come on, Em," she said. "There's plenty of room in here."

Emery followed his sister, handing her his things before wriggling through the opening. Evie shut the tiny panel just as two crew members walked past.

Evie pulled out her TAB computer to use as a light. The twins found an empty corner in the crate and slid to the floor. Then, they heard a loud creaking sound. The crate rose into the air. It tilted, slamming the twins back against the wall.

Evie clapped a hand over her mouth to hold back a yelp. Emery glared a warning at her.

"Someone didn't pack this crate right," a voice called from the outside. "It's too heavy on one side."

The crate landed inside the barge with a heavy *thud*. The voice shouted some commands, and then there was silence. The twins heard a few more crates being loaded on, and finally, the slow screech of heavy doors.

The star-barge was ready to launch.

The barge powered up with a low rumble.
Within minutes, they were floating in space.
Soon the main thruster engines would turn on
and take them to the planet.

"Do you think it'll be loud?" Evie whispered
to her brother. They'd never been on a star-barge
before. "I've heard some of the crew say that the
engines sound like giants waking up from a deep
sleep."

"You really do have a wild imagination,"
Emery said. "It's just a regular ship that makes
regular engine noises. They should be firing
them up right about now."

Exactly on cue, the crate vibrated from top
to bottom. Evie could feel her bones shaking.
She scrambled closer to her brother and hung
on to his arm. He clutched her hand.

For several seconds, the roar of the thrusters was so loud that Evie couldn't hear her own thoughts. But the engines steadied, and the noise quieted to a dull hum.

They were on their way toward the planet. Evie let out a breath.

"How long will this take?" she asked Emery.

He shrugged. "I'm guessing a couple of hours. Are you OK?"

Evie nodded. She patted her life-pack, just to reassure herself that she had brought everything she would need.

Evie was about to ask Emery where they should look first when they arrived on the planet. But she heard voices and shuffling. It was some of the crew, settling around the equipment for the ride. They were chatting about the trip.

"I sure hope this planet is the one," said a man with a low voice. "I'm sick of doing these missions."

"You don't like checking out new planets?" another man said. He sounded much younger.

"From far away, sure," the first man said. "But up close, these places can be terrifying."

A woman chimed in. "What's the worst place you've explored?"

The first man laughed. "I've been to planets where the air was so toxic, even our Spaceskins didn't protect us. Almost died on that trip." He paused. It sounded like he was drinking something. "Then there was the one where the life-forms didn't show up on our scanners. We almost settled there, until the creatures ambushed the building team. We lost three crew that day. Bloodiest thing I've ever seen."

There were murmurs from several other voices. Evie looked at Emery.

"See?" she whispered. "Our scanners can't find everything. There could be life on the planet."

"*Shhh*," her brother replied.

"I heard there was a planet where the crew was attacked by something they couldn't see," the woman said. "They were all sick for days."

The first man laughed again. "I didn't go on that trip, but I saw the crew when they got back. One of them kept moaning about ghosts."

"I remember that," another woman said. "You know, people used to believe that if you disturbed an ancient burial site, the ghosts of the dead would haunt you. I always thought those legends were nonsense, until that crew came back. Now I'm not so sure."

Emery shook his head as the twins listened. "Don't let them scare you," he whispered to Evie. "That's just a story. I read the actual reports. Medics said an alien virus caused hallucinations. The crew was just seeing things."

Evie shivered. She didn't want to hear any of this. They were heading down to a planet they barely knew anything about. There could be poisoned air, or aliens that didn't show up on scanners. And if life had existed on this planet a long time ago, maybe there were ghosts too.

Evie groaned quietly as she leaned against the crate. Why did she agree to her brother's suggestion to sneak onto a star-barge? What made her do something so stupid?

4

The crew of the star-barge finished unloading all the crates onto the planet surface within ten minutes of landing. Evie and Emery heard them leave. They were going off to have their meal back on the barge.

For the first time in hours, the twins dared to stand up and stretch.

"I'm glad we have our Spaceskins on," Emery said. His voice sounded digital as it came through the helmet's speaker. "I didn't think they'd unload the equipment so quickly."

"I guess my wild imagination has some advantages," Evie said with a smile.

It had been her idea to suit up before they landed. She wanted to be protected from invisible aliens, strange viruses, or any other horrors that awaited them.

The twins checked each other's suits to make sure there were no leaks. The Spaceskins stuck to their bodies like a second skin, while gold and blue tubing snaked around them. These tubes gave them the right amount of pressure and breathable air. It even recycled fluids to keep them hydrated.

And attached to each helmet was a tiny camera. It had started recording their journey the moment they turned on the suit.

"OK, let's get going. I'll have to open the entire side of the crate," Evie said. "Our helmets won't fit through the small door."

"How will you do that?" Emery asked.

Evie grinned. "I studied these crates in one of my units. I thought about joining the cargo crew once. Then I decided it would be too boring."

Evie climbed around the chunks of building material tied down in the middle of the crate. Then she started searching the wall.

"There should be a control panel in here. It's for when crew need to unload heavier cargo," she said. "They can control the floor ramp from inside the crate. It's pretty clever, really."

"Enough talking and more doing," Emery said. He knew that when his sister was nervous, she started to talk a lot.

Evie finally found the control panel. She opened the side of the crate, and the twins stepped into the glaring sunlight of the planet AX-351.

Evie squinted and gasped as she looked up. She'd never seen a sky before. Her whole life had been spent aboard the *Wanderer*. She didn't expect the colors she saw: clear blue and a rich orange.

"It's nothing like the picture in the archives!" she exclaimed. "I never imagined the sky would be so big. It just stretches on and on."

Emery stomped his boots on the bright green grass. "Natural gravity is so different too," he said. "Just look at how the grass springs back up after I've stepped on it!"

The sound of approaching voices broke them out of their moment of awe. The twins picked up their life-packs and ran to a cluster of trees.

When they were safely out of sight, they stopped to catch their breath. Running in real gravity was hard. And their bubble-like helmets were heavy.

Emery took out his TAB computer and pulled up a map of the area. He pointed toward a thick forest.

"We should go that way," he said. "There's a clearing beyond the trees. It'll be perfect for gathering samples."

"What about *my* mission?" Evie asked him. "I thought you were going to help me find evidence of life."

Emery was already several steps ahead of Evie. "My work will be faster," he said. "We'll do it first and then we'll do what you want."

As they went into the forest, Evie couldn't stop staring at the trees. They were nothing like the ones that grew on the *Wanderer*'s Airdeck, where the botanists kept samples of Earth plants. Those trees were small and skinny, with pale green leaves.

But the trees on AX-351 were enormous and majestic. Their thick trunks were a light brown color and smoother than Evie's TAB screen.

The twins walked through the forest for a while. There wasn't a lot of light because the trees were so tall, and their branches crisscrossed at the top to form a canopy. It was as if a large umbrella of leaves was shielding the twins from the glaring sunlight.

Soon the trees opened into a grassy area. Emery jogged into the middle of the clearing.

"This is perfect!" Emery said. He knelt down and opened up his pack. "I can get more than ten samples from just this spot."

Emery pulled out a boxy object. It was his BotanyBot. He had made the special computer himself three years ago. He had already used it to analyze every plant on the Airdeck.

Evie knew that when Emery got started with the BotanyBot, nothing would tear him away. So, she kept walking ahead. Maybe she would find something useful for her project.

On the other side of the clearing, she noticed the trees were a little different. They were slim, their bark was rough, and they had pointy leaves. When she looked closely, she found strange plants growing on their trunks.

She bent down to examine the odd plants. They had stubby stems that were almost white. They split into branches, like vines, as they grew upward against the tree. The higher they went, the thinner and messier the branches became.

It reminded Evie of human blood vessels.

"Emery will want a sample of this," Evie said to herself. She pulled out her pocketknife and sawed off a section of the vine.

A deep purple sap immediately oozed from the cut and onto her glove.

"Ugh!" Evie cried, pulling back. Dripping off her glove, the liquid looked like blood.

She shook her hand to try to fling off the sap. A few drops splattered against her helmet.

Her stomach cramped, and her dinner almost came back up. But she couldn't afford to throw up inside her helmet. She closed her eyes and took deep breaths until her stomach calmed down.

When she reopened her eyes, the vine she'd cut off was snaking itself around her left glove. Evie stared in disbelief.

It wove around her wrist and then slithered down to her palm. The vine split into two, then four, then eight. It began to branch out like it had on the tree trunk. Except now it was covering Evie's palm.

With her other hand, Evie pulled at the vines. But they wouldn't budge. Tiny thorns dug into the fabric of her glove.

Her heart began to race. She tried to call out to Emery, but her voice caught in her throat.

"Hey, Evie," she heard Emery say. "You need to look at this. I've never seen anything like these plants."

Evie tugged as the vine twisted around her fingers. It was almost strangling her entire hand now. She stomped her feet, trying to catch Emery's attention. But he was so focused on his work that he hadn't even looked up when he spoke to her.

As the vine reached her fingertips, Evie's vision became blurry. Had the thorns poked through her Spaceskin? Was she leaking air?

Evie yanked with all her might, scared now that she might black out.

"I'm beginning to think—" Emery didn't finish his sentence.

Evie took a deep breath and forced out a scream that echoed across the clearing. Emery jumped up and came running.

Just as he reached his sister, the vine relaxed and fell right off Evie's hand. It lay quiet on the ground, like a dead plant.

"What?" Emery sounded panicked. "Are you all right?"

"That thing!" Evie cried finally. "It tried to get in my suit!" She checked her glove for holes, but she didn't see any.

Emery picked up the vine. It didn't move.

"Well, it's not trying to attack me," he said. He looked at it more closely. "Amazing. This plant is even more unusual than the one I found."

He turned and started walking back to his BotanyBot.

"Em, put that down!" Evie said. "It isn't a regular plant!"

"Uh-huh," Emery mumbled. He held up the vine to look at it in the sunlight. "Now I'm going to win the internship for sure."

Evie ran after Emery. She grabbed his shoulder and turned him around.

"No, really," she said, trying her best not to sound like she was whining. He wouldn't take her seriously if she was whining. "That thing tried to strangle my hand."

Emery sighed. "Ev, you're probably still a little freaked out by those stories the crew told on board the star-barge. This is all just your imagination."

Evie's face grew hot. "I didn't imagine it! That plant was spreading over me like a spider web. You need to be careful."

"Enough!" Emery snapped. He shrugged her hand off his shoulder and went back to his BotanyBot. "We need to finish up and get back to the star-barge as soon as we can."

"But what about looking for evidence of life?" Evie called after her twin.

Emery didn't even turn around. He got right back to work with his samples. He didn't care about Evie's project. And he didn't believe a word she'd said.

For a moment, Evie felt helpless. Then, she just got mad.

Fine, she thought. *Get your samples. I'm going to find my evidence. By myself.*

She was going to prove there was intelligent life on this planet, and that the *Wanderer* crew shouldn't start building their new home wherever they wanted.

Evie stomped back toward the slim trees and the vines. She was careful not to touch any. She kept walking through the forest until she came to another clearing.

Grass didn't grow here, though. The ground was reddish brown, dusty, and dry. It was such a contrast to the green area where Emery was working.

But in the dirt, Evie saw something familiar. Something she'd seen in the holo-images taken by the drones. It made the hairs on the back of her neck stand straight up.

Footprints!

Scattered around the ground in front of Evie were a trail of footprints. She bent down and ran her hand over a print.

It was squarish and about the length of her pinky finger. Six tiny dots lined the front of the square. That meant whatever made these had claws. The prints also went deep into the ground. So the creatures was heavy, had six toes, and maybe four legs. Or eight.

Evie couldn't really tell, there were so many prints.

She touched the right side of her helmet, where the Spaceskin's camera control panel was. Her suit had been recording every step she'd taken since she'd put it on. But she needed to take holo-images of this important discovery.

On the inside of her helmet, an extra screen popped up. She zoomed the holo-camera in on the footprints.

Her hand was shaking, and the first few shots were blurry. She had the focus all wrong.

"Deep breaths," she reminded herself.

She was excited, but her brother's voice echoed in her mind. He'd say it was her wild imagination and that they were nothing more than natural land formations. She needed solid proof that would convince everyone.

She shook out her hands and tried again. This time, she got clear images.

A gust of wind whooshed by. Dust swirled off the ground, and in seconds the footprints disappeared. Evie tried to gently brush away the top layer of dust, but the prints had been smudged.

The footprints didn't look like footprints anymore. They looked like blotches in the dirt.

Evie sighed and pulled out her TAB. She started uploading the holo-images she'd taken to the device. Then something darted in the corner of her vision.

She turned just as a shadow scuttled across the ground and disappeared behind a pile of rocks. She didn't get a good look, but it had to be some kind of animal. The fresh footprints proved it!

"There you are!" Evie whispered. Her heart skipped a beat as she touched the new six-toed prints. "I knew you existed."

She ran after the creature toward the pile of rocks. She tried to dig her hands into the tiny space it had disappeared into, but her gloves were too thick. She managed to pull away a few rocks, but most of them were firmly stuck to each other or the ground.

Evie grunted in frustration. She was so close to getting proof of an actual, living creature. She couldn't give up now.

She walked around the mound of rocks. On the other side, she noticed a slightly larger opening. It was completely black, as if it led somewhere deep underground.

She bent down and peered inside, but she saw nothing. She tried to squeeze through, but her helmet was too big.

"This is ridiculous!" Evie exclaimed. She sat on the ground and tried to come up with a plan.

This planet was the most Earth-like one they had ever found. Everyone on the *Wanderer* said so. That was why there was so much excitement on board.

Evie pulled out her TAB. "Analyze the air," she told it.

In seconds, her TAB replied, "Air is within acceptable limits for humans."

The air was breathable. But Evie knew the rules. Never remove your helmet without the captain's approval.

She stared at the footprints and the rocks again. Maybe she *was* imagining things.

"No," she told herself. "What I saw was real."

She looked around to see if Emery had come looking for her. But he was nowhere to be seen. She turned back to the hole in the rocks.

Suddenly a sharp scratching sound echoed in the dark. Something was definitely moving inside.

Evie picked up her TAB and checked the air again. The words AIR BREATHABLE flashed across the screen.

Finally, she unclipped the locks on her helmet and pulled it off.

Evie took a deep breath. The air smelled funny, like Emery after his workouts. But she didn't feel dizzy or sick.

The TAB had been right. The air was safe.

So, Evie slipped out of her Spaceskin and carefully placed it on the ground. The heat from the sun warmed her bare arms and legs. She'd never felt that before. It was a good feeling.

But she didn't have time to enjoy it. She had to enter the black hole.

Evie unclipped the camera from her helmet, grabbed her flashlight, and crawled into the opening. The farther she went, the bigger the hole became. After a while, it opened up into a cave.

The cave was dark and cold and so big that the whole crew of the *Wanderer* could have fit inside. Every step Evie took seemed to rumble like distant thunder. Even her breaths sounded loud in the large, empty space.

"Don't be scared," Evie said to herself. "There is life here. And I'm going to prove it."

She aimed her light across the dark floor. There were more footprints here—lots more. She held up the camera and started taking holo-images.

When Evie was done, she sat down on a rock. She had some good evidence, but she really wanted a photo of an actual animal. They must be hiding from her.

She worked on quieting her breathing. She stayed as still as she could. Maybe the creatures would think she'd left, and they would come out.

After a minute of silence, Evie heard scuttling behind her. She slowly turned, with her camera ready. There was nothing there.

Then a long, low noise swept through the cave. It sounded like a groan. It sounded humanlike.

Evie whipped back around, but all she saw was emptiness.

"H-hello? Em?" she said.

Evie's heart was thumping in her chest. She slid off the rock and hid behind it. "This isn't funny, Emery," she said. "Show yourself!"

No one answered. The only sound in the cave was her panting.

Then she remembered the story she'd heard on the star-barge—about disturbing burial sites. What if aliens had been buried in this cave? Had she awakened their ghosts?

"No, I just imagined the sound," Evie said to herself. She leaned her face against the smooth, cool rock. "There's no one here."

A shrill screech suddenly filled the entire cave. It bounced off the walls and echoed wildly. It was as if a hundred voices were screaming all at once.

Evie jumped up and rushed outside. As she scrambled through the tunnel, she bumped into the rocky wall. A sharp edge cut into her arm. She didn't care. She just wanted to get out.

Once she staggered outside, she noticed that the sky had gotten darker. It was more burnt orange than blue now. The air smelled even more like sweat.

Evie grabbed her Spaceskin and headed for Emery. She pulled her suit back on as she stumbled toward the forest.

She had to warn the crew. She had to tell them something was wrong with this planet.

Her heart was pounding like a loud drum, so she didn't notice the other sounds at first. But just as she was putting her helmet back on, she heard it.

Groans and screeching.

The sounds were louder outside the cave, and they were getting louder with each step she took. Evie didn't dare turn around. She ran.

Whatever had been inside the cave was now outside.

6

"People used to believe that if you disturbed an ancient burial site, the ghosts of the dead would haunt you."

The words kept repeating themselves in Evie's mind as she ran to find her brother. It mixed with the ghostly sounds behind her. The flurry of noises made her head hurt.

When she finally reached the trees, Evie called out. "Emery!"

She paused to listen. There was no answer.

And she couldn't hear the moans from the ghosts either. The forest was suddenly silent. Had she outrun them?

Evie searched and searched for Emery, trying to remember the location of the clearing. Then, she saw something ahead.

Emery was lying on the ground—without his Spaceskin.

"Em! Are you all right?" Evie cried, pushing herself to move faster.

He didn't reply.

Evie sprinted to her brother's side. Emery was lying next to the trees where she had found the strange white plants. The plants' branches had spread out like a net over Emery's bare wrists and ankles. They were holding him to the ground.

Did the plants pull him out of his Spaceskin?
Evie wondered in panic. He would never take
it off willingly.

But Emery wasn't fighting the plants as they
crept over him. He just stared at the treetops.

"Em!" Evie shrieked. "Emery, say something!"

She dropped down and began to tear at the
plant, but she could barely get her fingers around
the thin branches. Her gloves were so thick that
she couldn't grip them.

Her twin turned his face toward her. His eyes
were the exact color of the blades of grass. They
were bright green.

Evie stumbled back. *What is going on?*

She had to hurry. Patting her Spaceskin, she
pulled out the pocketknife. She began to saw at
the vine around his arm.

When Evie made the first cut, the dark
blood-like liquid oozed from the plant.

Emery twitched and groaned. He sounded
exactly like the ghosts in the cave.

"Am I hurting you, Em?" Evie asked. He didn't
answer. She cut deeper until the vine broke off.
"I'm sorry. I have to get you free. Help me pull
you away."

Emery didn't answer, and he didn't help her.
He just stared at her with his strange-colored eyes.

When Evie cut through a second vine,
Emery hissed at her. His teeth were sharp, like
animal fangs.

Evie screamed and scrambled away. Emery
hissed again. But he didn't say a word. It was as
if he had forgotten how to talk.

"No, Em!" Evie began to cry. "Stay with me!"

Crying inside a Spaceskin helmet was a bad thing to do. The moisture was fogging up the front. Evie removed the helmet and swiped at her nose with a gloved hand.

What was she going to do?

"Please," Emery whimpered. Evie looked up, shocked. Emery was still staring at her, but he seemed to recognize her now. "Help . . . me."

"Em?" Evie whispered. She came closer, touching his arm.

But then the wild look came back into his bright green eyes. Emery let out a sharp hiss. He bared his fangs.

Evie pulled her hand back. She was terrified of her own twin. He was turning into something strange. But his real self was still in there. She had to save him.

She grabbed the knife and began sawing again. She ignored his moans and hissing this time.

But when she cut off one branch, another appeared and curled around her brother. They held him tight against the ground.

"We should've never come here," she sobbed.

Evie kept sawing through the plants. The plants kept growing back.

"I'll save you. I'll save you," she repeated through tears and hiccups.

Finally Evie had to stop to take a breath. She stared in horror at the pool of dark purple liquid around her from all the vines she had hacked away. Yet Emery was still covered in the plants.

She wasn't going to be able to do this by herself. She needed to find help.

Evie got to her feet and clipped on her helmet back on. She looked down at her brother. "I'll be back soon," she promised. "Just hold on, OK?"

Emery hissed. His sharp teeth and bright green eyes sent shivers up and down her spine.

Evie ran toward the building site. She could hear the voices of the crew before she saw them. They were taking out equipment from the crates.

"Help!" Evie shouted, waving her arms.

But no one responded. They didn't even turn around.

Evie kept calling for help as she ran. She didn't understand why the crew wasn't reacting to her cries. Couldn't they hear her?

Suddenly Evie's foot caught against something. With a painful thud, she hit the ground. Then she rolled, over and over.

She was tumbling downhill, and she couldn't stop. She could feel each bump and sharp stone. They dug through her suit and into her skin.

When she finally landed at the bottom of the hill, Evie felt as if her skin was on fire. Her suit had barely protected her.

"Ow!" she moaned. "Ow! Ow! Ow!"

She slid out of her Spaceskin to check on the most painful spots. Tiny red splotches were scattered along her arms and legs. She rubbed them. They began to blister.

"What?" she cried.

Each splotch turned into little bubbles on her skin. They burned like boiling water. They hurt so much, tears started streaming down her cheeks.

"Help!" Evie yelled again. She was sobbing now. Surely one of the crew would hear her.

But the only answer she received was the sound of moaning.

The ghosts of the cave were back, and they'd found her.

7

Evie tried to get back onto her feet. She had to get away from the ghosts. She had to find help for Emery. She had to warn the rest of the crew.

But her legs wouldn't move. Worse, with every attempt to stand, more boils popped up on her shins, her knees, her thighs.

Evie shut her eyes tightly. *This isn't possible. It's all just a bad dream*, she thought. *I'm in bed on board the* Wanderer. *This is nothing more than a terrible nightmare.*

The moans grew longer and louder. They were getting closer.

Evie couldn't help it. She opened one eye. What she saw made her heart jump into her throat.

Lumbering toward her were huge creatures. Dozens of curving tendrils waved and wriggled out from them. The things moved just above the ground, like the crates that hovered into the star-barge. As they floated closer, loud moans and screeches pierced the air.

Evie couldn't make out a face or mouth on the creatures. How were they making sounds? Yet the ear-splitting groans definitely came from these alien beings.

As they got closer to her, the sun shone through their greenish bodies. Through them!

"They *are* ghosts!" she cried.

"Why . . ." The word floated in the air between the ghostly creatures and Evie. "Why . . . are . . . you . . . here?"

The question rang so clearly in her ears. *They speak our language?* Evie thought. *How?*

She tried to stand again, but her legs simply wouldn't obey. More boils grew on her skin, and the pain just got worse.

The ghosts moved closer. Their one question kept repeating itself, over and over: *Why are you here? Why are you here? Why are you here?*

Evie pressed her hands to her ears, but that didn't help. She could hear them inside her head.

"Stop!" she yelled.

And surprisingly, they did. Evie looked up at the circle of ghosts surrounding her. It was like being in the middle of a glass forest.

Beyond the ghosts, Evie's eyes caught sight of something in the sky. Another star-barge was landing. Her mom would be on that one.

Mom would help her. And Emery. Evie thought of her brother, tangled in the vines, and her heart sank. What if help didn't arrive in time? She had to do something now.

"We're not here to hurt you," she said to the aliens. "Please believe me!"

The ghosts made a sound like sighing. "You hurt our babies," they said.

"What babies?" Evie didn't remember seeing anything like a baby. "What are you?"

"Why are you here?" they repeated.

Evie crossed her arms, but touching her own skin hurt. She uncrossed them. Maybe the best way out of this was to tell the truth.

"We're humans, from a planet called Earth. Our planet was destroyed," Evie explained. "We're looking for a new home."

She tried to sound calm even though her heart was beating wildly. "Our scanners showed no one was living here. We wouldn't take your children or your planet, if we knew you were here."

"No, no, no!" they all moaned.

"Please, let me go," Evie said.

"Go, go, go," the ghosts echoed.

"If you let me go, I'll tell my people you're here, and we'll leave. I promise!" She knew that was a lie. She was a twelve, and who believed the twelves? Still, she would try to keep her promise.

The alien ghosts started talking all at once. Each one was saying something different. Evie couldn't understand anything.

Suddenly the ghosts' waving tendrils started swatting at Evie. They scratched her already sore skin.

"No, please!" Evie cried.

She grabbed one of the tendrils before it could hit her again. She gasped in pain, and up close she could see the tendril had nasty-looking spikes all along it.

Then, as she gripped the tendril, Evie realized—these things weren't ghosts after all.

The aliens were real and solid, even if they were see-through. And they were angry with her.

Something else touched her back. Evie twisted around to see a whole army of boils closing in on her.

Walking boils? Evie blinked and looked again.

They were some kind of bug that looked like the boils on her skin. They had too many legs to count and large domed bodies that glowed a glassy, pinkish red. The bugs skittered across the ground, and they were coming for her.

Evie opened her mouth to scream, but the aliens' voices drowned her out. Hundreds of domed bugs crawled toward her, slipping through the circle of aliens.

They wriggled underneath her and lifted her off the ground. The aliens turned away from the building site, leading the bugs and Evie back toward the cave.

8

The bugs carried Evie through the forest.
Emery had to be in there somewhere. Evie tried
to lift her head to search for him, but she couldn't
move her body. She felt as if she was a main course,
being served to aliens on a walking tray of bugs.
Yet she couldn't even scream.

When they passed by the skinny trees with the
white vines, the aliens stopped. They bent down
next to the trunks. From what little Evie could see,
it looked as though the aliens were gently stroking
the cluster of white plants.

"Our babies." The words floated in Evie's head.

Evie's mind raced. *Those plants are their children?* she thought.

All at once she could see the similarities. The see-through aliens' tendrils were just much larger versions of the thin branches on the white plants. Except they weren't really plants. They were alien beings. Or maybe they were both.

Evie suddenly remembered how she'd cut through the vines. She remembered the dark liquid that had oozed from them.

Had she destroyed some of their young? Is that why she was being punished?

Evie wanted to say she was sorry. That she had no idea. But she couldn't open her mouth. She had tried to stop humans from harming the life on this planet. Now, she was the guilty one.

Tears flowed fast and freely down Evie's face. They plopped onto the domed bugs. Every time a tear hit one, she heard a hiss, like the sound of lab-grown bacon sizzling in the microwave.

The bugs carried Evie on toward the cave. The aliens followed, some carrying the young in their vine-like arms. Without warning, the bugs dropped Evie down onto the ground with a *thud*. They scuttled away into the rocks.

The aliens surrounded Evie once more. This time, they spoke with one voice. "You hurt our babies. Now you feed them."

Before she could even say anything, the aliens placed the small white clusters of vines on Evie's arms and legs. She felt tiny thorns pierce her skin. It hurt, but only for a moment.

Then, Evie simply felt tired. She just wanted to sleep.

Evie thought of her twin as blackness filled her vision. This must've been what happened to Emery. The plants were slowly eating him too. At least he didn't feel any pain either. That much was good.

Evie's body began to rock from side to side. Something was shaking her. She kept her eyes squeezed shut. She didn't want to watch herself being eaten up. Then the something called her name.

"Evie, are you OK?" it asked.

That was Emery. Evie opened her eyes.

There was her twin, looking down at her. Emery's eyes were still bright green, but he was alive. And he was back in his Spaceskin. Evie looked around.

She was lying by the pile of rocks, where she had first spotted the footprints. Her Spaceskin lay neatly folded next to her. There was no sign of the aliens or the bugs. No baby plants sucking the life out of her.

She looked down at her arms. Red spots dotted her skin, but they were nothing like the large boils she remembered.

"Oh, Em," Evie cried. Her voice was back. "I was so scared. How did you get away?"

Emery frowned. "What are you talking about?"

"Aliens were eating . . ." Evie trailed off.

Emery's frown was slowly turning into an ugly grin. He picked up something. "Here," he said. "You need this."

It was a young alien. Its tiny vines wriggled eagerly as Emery placed it on her legs.

"No!" Evie screamed. She felt the thorns prick her skin. "Stop! What are you doing?"

"It's for your own good," Emery said with a wicked gleam in his eyes.

Evie couldn't understand why her twin was trying to hurt her. Somehow, her arms were able to move again. She shoved Emery with all her might, and he fell back.

"Hey! Knock that off!" Emery cried.

Evie tried to run, but she couldn't stand up. Her legs were held down to the ground with alien baby plants. Her waist too. She started pulling at them when two familiar faces popped into view.

"Mom! Dad!" Evie yelled. She was so glad to see them. She was saved.

But something was wrong with her parents. They had young alien vines in their hands too.

"Don't move, Evie dear," Mom said. She used the vines to pin down Evie's arms.

"This has to be done," Dad added.

Evie stared in disbelief. Her parents were on the aliens' side too? This had to be a trick of her mind. The aliens must be able to make her see things that weren't real.

Dad picked up another baby alien. Evie saw the sharp thorns dangling over her face. Dad was going to put it right on her neck. Mom was doing the same thing on her other side.

Evie tried to struggle, but she was completely tied down.

"Stay still," Dad ordered. His voice sounded funny and far away.

The thorns pierced Evie's neck. She could feel something warm enter her body.

The sky above swirled orange, pink, green, and blue. If she wasn't so scared, Evie would've thought it was the most beautiful thing she'd ever seen.

Evie suddenly felt very, very sleepy.

This was her end. She had hurt alien creatures. And her family was helping the aliens punish her for what she'd done.

Evie thought it was unfair that her family didn't try to save her, but she was too tired to be angry, or sad, or scared.

So Evie gave up. She shut her eyes and wondered what would come next. The last thing she heard was the whispering voices of the aliens. They were chanting.

"Food. Food. Good food."

9

A familiar rhythm tapped inside Evie's brain. It blossomed into a sweet melody. Evie hummed along. It was a song she knew well. Dad used to sing it to her at bedtime.

Her dad. Her dad who had betrayed her and fed her to the aliens.

Evie tried to open her eyes, but everything was blurry. Her eyes felt sore. In fact, her whole body was sore, right down to her toes. She groaned.

She knew, though, that she wasn't lying on the ground anymore. The surface beneath her was soft.

Evie blinked until the room came into focus. She was in the sick bay, in a hospital bed.

Tubes stretched from her arms to three medical bots. There was one on each side of her and one on the ceiling. The ceiling bot also had several pointy sensors aimed down at her. It hummed softly as it scanned her. Somewhere in the room, she heard muffled voices.

Slowly, Evie turned her head. Emery was asleep in a chair beside her bed.

Evie jerked. He had tried to feed her to the aliens! She struggled against the straps that held her to the bed.

"You're awake!" Emery exclaimed. He jumped out of his chair and rushed to her side.

Evie stiffened. She stared at her twin. His eyes were no longer bright green. They were back to his usual brown with tiny greenish specks.

But what if the monster was just hiding inside? What if he turned evil again?

"It's all right," Emery said, laying a gentle hand on her arm. "You're safe now. You're back on the *Wanderer.*"

Evie was silent for a moment. Then she asked, "What happened?" Her voice came out like a croak, as if she hadn't spoken in a long time.

Emery looked over to the other side of the room. Evie followed his eyes. Their parents were there, talking to a medic. Emery sighed.

"I found you by some rocks," he said. "You were unconscious, and you weren't in your Spaceskin. Why would you take it off?"

Evie didn't want to tell him about the aliens and bugs. She wasn't sure he'd believe her. She wasn't sure she believed herself.

Her brain felt so fuzzy. She couldn't figure out what was real and what wasn't. She looked at her arms. There were no boils, only small red splotches.

"It looks like you were bitten by something, doesn't it?" Emery said, noticing her gaze.

"Bitten?" Evie's breaths came fast as she remembered the aliens' thorns.

"Don't worry," Emery said. "We didn't find anything that could've done it. The medics say the spots are probably a reaction to something on the planet."

"But I *was* bitten," Evie said. Emery didn't seem to have any memory of what had happened. "You were too. How did you get free?"

"I don't know what you mean," Emery said. "I'm fine. But when I found you, I couldn't wake you. So I ran for help. Mom's barge had just landed. We got you on board, and I had to hold you down while the medics stuck all these tubes in you."

Evie shook her head. She had vague memories of Emery trying to stick young aliens on her skin. Were they actually just medics' needles?

"You struggled a lot, even though you weren't awake. It was the strangest thing," Emery said. "You've been out for days."

"Days?" Evie murmured.

"Yes, three ship-days to be exact," a voice said. Dad had appeared at the other side of Evie's bed. Mom stood next to Emery.

Evie's heart raced as her parents squeezed her hands. Were they going to harm her, or were they here to help? Everything was so confusing.

But these parents didn't look evil. They just seemed worried. Evie relaxed a little more.

"What were you thinking, going down to the planet on your own?" Mom asked.

"I'm so sorry, Mom and Dad," Evie whispered. She didn't care if they grounded her for life. She was so glad to be home.

"The medics think you were poisoned by something that scratched you," Dad said. "Why would you get out of your Spaceskin? You know it's not safe."

"I saw something. The TAB said the air was breathable . . ." Evie's voice drifted off.

"The air might be OK, but there could be other things we know nothing about," Dad said. "It's an alien planet, after all. We're still discovering its secrets."

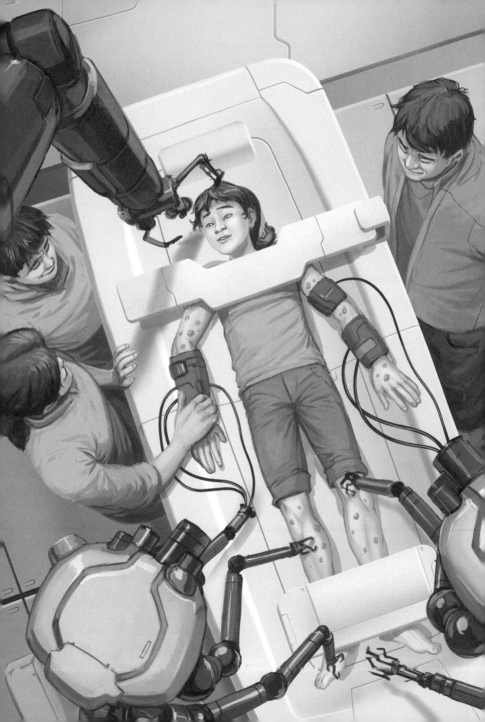

"The most important thing is that you're safe now," Mom added.

"Hey, this'll make you happy," Emery said. "We found the holo-images on your TAB. The ones you took of the footprints. Looks like you were right. There might be life on the surface after all."

Mom nodded. "So the captain has stopped all work on the ground. He thinks we need to study the planet more before we decide whether to stay. This may not be the world for us."

Evie couldn't believe her ears. She had done what she set out to do. The *Wanderer* was going to leave!

Then something came to her mind. "What about the video from my Spaceskin?" she asked. The camera recorded everything. It would show her which experiences were real and which were not. "Did you see anything . . . weird?"

Dad shook his head. "The memory chip was missing," he said. "It must've fallen out when you took off the suit."

"Oh," Evie said, disappointed. She would have to sort through her memories herself.

"We should let you rest," Mom said. "We'll see you after our shifts." She gave Evie a kiss and then went back with Dad to talk to the medic.

Emery stayed by her side. Evie looked at him carefully. His eyes were still brown. Maybe everything really was back to normal.

"Are we in trouble?" she asked her brother.

He shook his head. "The captain was mad. But your images and my analysis of the plant life were so useful, he forgave us for sneaking off the ship."

Evie was relieved. "What did your analysis show?"

Emery grinned with pride. "I cataloged over twenty plant species. Most were pretty ordinary. But that one plant, the one you found . . ."

"The white ones with the vines?" Evie's heart sped up.

"Yeah, those," Emery said. "They're not just plants. They have elements of plant *and* animal in them. They're fascinating. They start out a really light green color, but as they grow they become almost see-through. The chief botanist also discovered they have a sap that can mess with our minds. It makes us see things that aren't there. That might be what poisoned you."

Evie's stomach started to twist. Maybe that purple sap had gotten through her gloves when she first cut the white vines. She could have imagined everything.

On the other hand, what if the aliens were real?

The poison seemed like a good way for them to terrify their victims. Once people were scared and confused, the aliens could easily gobble them up.

Then, something clicked in Evie's brain to make her panic all over again.

"What do you mean the chief botanist found this out?" Evie asked. "Didn't you analyze the plant with your BotanyBot while you were on the planet?"

Emery leaned in closer. "I brought a young cluster up to the ship. They're in the lab."

"No!" Evie croaked. "Take them back!"

"Don't worry!" Emery said. He looked shocked. "I only took a small sample. It's no big deal. We keep them in a sealed lab. Especially because the sap is poisonous."

Evie inhaled too quickly and couldn't stop coughing. Emery tried to calm her, but she needed to tell him. He needed to understand.

"We have to return those samples," Evie said, breathing heavily.

"Why?" Emery asked.

"Those plants are alien babies!"

10

The medics gave Evie drugs to keep her sleepy for the next few days. Every time she was awake enough, she remembered Emery had brought aliens onto the ship. When she tried to tell someone, they thought she was hallucinating. Then they made her go back to sleep.

So eventually, Evie gave up trying to warn them. Soon the medics allowed her family to visit.

"That poison really did some damage," Emery said as he sat next to Evie. "You've been saying strange things in your sleep."

"Like what?" Evie asked, trying her best to stay calm.

"It's nothing," Mom said. She gave Emery a stern look. "You were just having bad dreams."

"You kept talking about ghost aliens," Emery continued, ignoring their mom. "And how we'd stolen their children. Ghosts having kids—that would make an interesting story! Your imagination has been working overtime."

Evie took several deep breaths as Emery chuckled. She couldn't argue. No one would believe her.

"Hey, we have great news," Dad said. "The captain announced that we can still live on this planet. The construction work has begun."

"What?" Evie gasped. "I thought you said my evidence made them stop."

"It did," Mom said. "And you should be proud of yourself. We did more studies, but we found no evidence of creatures that made those footprints. The ship's zoologists think they had already died off long ago."

"If we ever do find other animals, though, we'll be respectful. I'm sure we can all live together peacefully," Dad said. Then he grinned. "But just think, we'll finally have a home planet! How exciting is that?"

Evie gave a weak smile as Mom and Dad went away to speak to the medics. Emery stayed with his sister.

"They also discovered that our white plants cover a large part of the planet," Emery told her. "If we avoid those areas and are careful, their poisonous sap won't harm anyone else. Thanks to you, we've learned how to stay safe."

Evie shook her head. This was all wrong. She had to tell someone that the plants *were* the native life-forms.

She didn't know why she was so sure. There wasn't any evidence. She could've imagined some of the strange things that happened on the planet. But something deep inside told her she was right about the aliens.

"Please, Em. Listen to me," she began. The machines she was hooked up to started to beep as her heart beat faster. She stopped and inhaled slowly. "I know it sounds weird. But those plants . . . they're . . ."

Emery put his hand on her arm. "It's OK, sis. We'll be safe." He tightened his grip. Her arm throbbed with pain.

"No, you're not listening," Evie said firmly. "The aliens will eat us . . ."

Emery leaned in closer. "That's your nightmare talking. It'll take a while for the poison to leave your system. In the meantime, you can't tell the difference between reality and fantasy. Would you like me to ask the medic to give you more medicine, to help you calm down?"

He'd said those words in a tone Evie had never heard before. It scared her.

"No, you're right," she whispered.

Emery let go of her arm. He patted her, as if she were a robotic pet. "Good. You rest and get better. I'm headed back to the lab to check on my babies."

Evie's heart skipped a beat. "What did you just say?"

Emery laughed. For a second, his eyes gleamed a bright green. Evie blinked, and her twin's eyes went back to normal.

"Sorry, I just meant my plant samples," he said. "They're kind of like my babies, since I'm taking care of them. You should see how much they've grown. They're doing really well aboard the ship."

A shiver ran right through Evie as she watched her brother walk away. What had happened to him? Had he really been caught up in the alien vines? Or was he telling the truth about her hallucinations?

Maybe it had all been a bad dream.

Or maybe the whole ship was in danger now.

EPILOGUE

On his way back to the botany lab, Emery stopped at their home quarters. Just as he walked into his bedroom, the all-ship announcement bell sounded. He stood in place and listened, as did everyone else on the ship.

It was the captain. "Crew of the *Wanderer*, this is an important day. After three generations of searching for a suitable planet, we have finally reached the end of our journey. I have contacted the other two ships—the *Explorer* and the *Hopeful*. They will meet us in three weeks."

He paused, and the whole ship heard him let out a relieved sigh. Emery smiled.

"When our ancestors fled a dying Earth, they dreamed of this day," the captain continued. "As one of the three starships carrying the last humans in the universe, we can be proud that we have finally found a planet where we can live. So, *Wanderer* crew, welcome to your new home."

The bell sounded again. The announcement was over.

Emery headed to his bed and pulled a box out from underneath. At the very bottom of the box was a pouch, and in the pouch was a memory chip.

He stuck the chip into his TAB. Emery touched the screen and a video played. He watched Evie being surrounded by the ghostly aliens, then by the bugs. Her Spaceskin had recorded her experiences.

Emery smiled to himself. He'd managed to grab the chip before the medics had reached her.

Emery watched his twin being carried away on the bugs. The see-through aliens gazed at Evie with curiosity. They were talking all at once.

With a swipe over the screen, Emery slowed the video down. Now he could clearly hear each alien.

"Delicious."

"Good source of food."

"So many of them."

"We'll grow and grow."

Emery swiped his hand over the screen again. A question appeared.

Delete or Save?

He put his finger on the *Delete* option.

Are you sure?

He pressed *Yes*.

The video fizzled out slowly. Emery's eyes
glowed a bright green. A grin curled his lips,
a curl like the tendril of a plant.

No one would ever know that Evie had been
right. Not even Evie herself. Emery's alien masters
would keep themselves hidden . . . until it was
time to feed.

INVISIBLE LIFE-FORMS

The ghosts that Evie sees on planet AX-351 turn out to be living beings, not dead ones. They are transparent, or see-through. In her life-form research, Evie might have learned that several creatures on Earth also have the same weird feature.

One of the most dramatic examples is the glasswing butterfly of Central and South America. The main part of each wing is clear as glass! This helps the butterfly escape predators—because hungry animals can look right at the insect and not even know it's there.

The eerie glass squid lives near the ocean's surface around the world. The squid appears as clear as the water surrounding it. Squids don't have sharp fangs or hard shells to defend themselves, so being almost invisible is a good way to avoid toothy sharks!

In the future special barriers might make buildings, spacecraft, and even people invisible too. Scientists have created mirrors and lenses that can "bend" light around an object. And if light doesn't hit you, then you can't be seen! Cloaking the *Wanderer* or its crew would come in handy when exploring dangerous new worlds. But remember . . . aliens could still smell you!

— *Michael*

GLOSSARY

analyze (AN-uh-lize)—to study something carefully in order to understand it

atmosphere (AT-muh-sfeer)—the layer of gases that surrounds a planet

barge (BARJ)—a large ship used to move objects

botanist (BAH-tuh-nist)—a scientist whose main focus is studying plants; botany is the study of plants

catalog (CAT-uh-log)—to describe and put into an organized list

disturb (dih-STURB)—to move or change something from its normal place

evidence (EV-uh-duhnss)—information, items, and facts that help prove something is true or false

hallucination (huh-loo-suh-NAY-shuhn)—something that is seen and heard but is not real

hologram (HOL-uh-gram)—a special type of image that looks solid and real, and is created with laser light

species (SPEE-sheez)—a group of plants or animals that share common features